P9-DTN-818

Hello—

I'm Emily Elizabeth.

If you don't live on my street,
you may not know me . . .

. . .or my dog Clifford.

He's a lot of fun to play with.

There is only one bad thing
about Clifford.

He eats a lot of dog food.
And a lot of dog food
costs a lot of money.

We were spending all our
money for dog food.
Mother and Daddy didn't
know what to do.
"We will have to send
Clifford away," they said.

Clifford didn't want to go away.
He made up his mind to get a job
and pay for his own dog food.

He decided to join the circus.
Good Old Clifford.

The circus man liked Clifford.
Clifford got the job.

But they put him in the side show.

He just sat there.

And people just looked at him.

Clifford wanted to do something.

He peeked into a tent.

He saw little dogs doing tricks.

Clifford wanted to do tricks too.

So he ran into the tent and he tried
to jump through the hoop—
just like the little dogs.

It didn't work.

In the next ring Clifford saw
a little dog riding on a pony.

Clifford thinks he can do
anything a little dog can do.

But he can't.

The circus man was angry.
He asked Clifford to leave.

"Don't worry," I said.
"You can get another job."

So we went to see a farmer.

The farmer thought Clifford
would be a good farm dog.
He said Clifford could
work for him.

First Clifford rounded up the cows.

Then Clifford brought home
a wagon full of hay.
He was doing so well . . .

And then he saw a rat
running to the barn.
Clifford knew that rats on
a farm are very bad!

So Clifford chased the rat.

Clifford and I started home.

We felt very bad.

Everything had gone wrong.

Suddenly a car came speeding past us.

And right behind it came a police car.

They were chasing robbers.

Clifford took a short cut
through the woods—

—and caught the robbers.

I was very proud.
The Chief of Police
offered Clifford a job
as a police dog.

Now Clifford goes to
work every day.
They don't pay him money.
But. . .

. . . every week they send
Clifford a lot of dog food.
So now we can keep him.
Isn't that wonderful?
Good Old Clifford.

NORMAN BRIDWELL

Clifford's
SPORTS DAY

BARNES
&NOBLE
BOOKS
NEW YORK

For Jennifer Naomi Morris

This edition published especially for Barnes & Noble by arrangement with Scholastic Inc.

1997 Barnes & Noble Books

ISBN 0-590-62971-9

Printed in the U.S.A.   24

First Scholastic printing, March 1996

I'm Emily Elizabeth. My dog is Clifford.

Last week I took him to school for our outdoor Sports Day.

Clifford had never gone to a Sports Day before.

The gym teachers had planned a day
full of races and games.

First was a sack race. Clifford wanted to try it.
The coach said that all his feet had to be in one bag.

I found a sack that was big enough.

Then we were off!

Clifford got an A for effort.

Next came the three-legged race

Clifford did better at that,
but the race was a little rough on me.

Clifford saw some kids jumping over hurdles.
It looked like fun.

Clifford took a running start....

He tried to jump all the hurdles at once!

CRASH! Jumping hurdles wasn't as easy as he thought.

The next event was tumbling.

Clifford was good at that.

He got a perfect 10.

Afterwards we had a tug-of-war.

Clifford saw that my side was in trouble.

He helped us out.

The other kids didn't like that.
They complained to the coach.

The coach said Clifford couldn't play anymore.

Our Sports Day was almost over by now
The last event was a softball game.
Clifford stayed to watch.

I knew he wanted to help our team,

but he obeyed the coach.

Even when the other team got a tremendous hit...

Clifford didn't try to catch the ball.

But he did catch the ball catcher,
just in time.

He didn't help us win the game...

...but he was the hero of our Sports Day.
Good work, Clifford!

NORMAN BRIDWELL

Clifford
THE FIREHOUSE DOG

BARNES
&NOBLE
BOOKS
NEW YORK

For Maxwell Bruno Wayne

This edition published especially for Barnes & Noble by arrangement with Scholastic Inc.

1997 Barnes & Noble Books

ISBN 0-590-48419-2

Printed in the U.S.A.   24

First Scholastic printing, September 1994

My name is Emily Elizabeth,
and this is my dog, Clifford.
Clifford is not the oldest in his family,
but he's the biggest.

Last week Clifford and I went to the city
to visit Clifford's brother, Nero.
Clifford knew the way.

Nero lives in a firehouse.
He is a fire rescue dog.

I asked the firefighters if Clifford could help them.
They thought he was the right color for the job.

Just then a group of schoolchildren came in
for a fire safety class.

Nero showed them what to do if their clothing was on fire.

To smother the flames, you stop,
drop to the floor,
and roll until the fire is out.

Clifford thought he could do that.
He repeated the lesson for the class.

He stopped.

He dropped.

He rolled.

He rolled a little too far.

Just then, we heard the siren.
There was a fire!

Nero stayed to guard the children.
Clifford and I ran ahead.

He cleared the street for the fire trucks.

Smoke was pouring from the top floor of a tall building. Clifford pushed the crowd back to a safe place.

He saw some people in trouble.

Clifford to the rescue!

The heavy hose was hard to unreel.
Clifford gave the firefighters a hand.

But then he saw that the fire hydrant was stuck shut.

Thank goodness Clifford was there to unstick it.

They had to get the smoke out of the building.
Clifford made a hole in the roof.

The firefighters were calling for more water.

Clifford found some.

He helped clear the smoke away.

When the fire was out, Clifford made sure that the firefighters got out of the building safely.

They were grateful for everything he had done to help.

We gave some firefighters a ride back to the firehouse.

Clifford was a hero! The fire chief made him an honorary fire rescue dog, just like his brother, Nero.

FIRE SAFETY RULES

1. Tape the number of your Fire Department to your telephone.*

2. Know two different ways out of your house or apartment building.

3. Choose a place nearby where you and other members of your family can meet if you have to leave your house and get separated.

4. Never go back into your house for anything if the building is on fire.

5. Tell your mom or dad to change the battery in your smoke alarms every year on your birthday.

6. Do NOT play with matches.

7. Never use the stove without an adult.

*Some phones can be programmed to dial the Fire Department for you. Ask your parents if your phone is programmed and how it works.

Clifford
TAKES A TRIP

Clifford
TAKES A TRIP

Story and pictures by Norman Bridwell

BARNES
&NOBLE
BOOKS
NEW YORK

To Tracy

This edition published especially for Barnes & Noble by arrangement with Scholastic Inc.

1997 Barnes & Noble Books

ISBN 0-590-44260-0

Printed in the U.S.A.

Hi, I'm Emily Elizabeth.
This is a happy day for me.

This is the last day of school.
Summer vacation is here!
Now I can play with my dog Clifford.

We don't go on long vacation trips.
It's too hard to get Clifford on a bus
or train.

We only go to places that Clifford can walk to, like picnics in the park.

Last year was different.
Last year we went to the mountains.
Mommy and Daddy said it was too far
for Clifford to walk.

So we left him with the lady next door.

That night Clifford was so lonely
he began to howl.
He howled and he howled
and he howled —

— until someone threw a shoe at him.
It didn't hurt Clifford's nose,
but it did hurt his feelings.

The next morning Clifford set out to find us.
He sniffed his way along the road.

Clifford didn't mean to make trouble.
But a lot of people had never seen
a big red dog before.

Clifford kept going.
Nothing could stop him.

And then he saw a little old man
trying to fix his truck.
The man needed help.

So Clifford stopped and helped him.
He took the little old man to a garage.

The little old man gave Clifford a little lunch,
to thank him for his help.

Then Clifford set out again.

Nothing stopped him — not even wet cement.

And traffic jams didn't stop him.
Clifford just tip-toed over the cars.
And then . . .

... he came to a toll bridge.
Clifford had no money.

But that didn't stop him.

We didn't know Clifford was coming.

I found some new playmates —
two baby bears.
I was having so much fun
I didn't see Mama Bear.

She didn't want strangers
to play with her babies.
She growled.
I was in real trouble.

Then we heard a LOUDER growl.
Guess who was growling!

Mama Bear was surprised.

She even forgot her babies.
I told Clifford that the Mama Bear
was only protecting her children.

Good old Clifford
took the baby bears
back to Mama Bear.

Then he took us all back to camp.
Mommy and Daddy were surprised
to see Clifford.

I told them how Clifford saved my life.

So they let Clifford stay with us.

Next year, maybe we will find a way
to take Clifford with us
when we go on vacation.